Hello, Victor E. Huskie™!

Ashley LePard

Illustrated by Cheri Nowak

MASCOT BOOKS®
www.mascotbooks.com

Fall had arrived in DeKalb, Illinois, and to the students of Northern Illinois University, that meant one thing … football season!

To kick off the first football game, Victor E. Huskie was making his way to the stadium, but he had a few stops to make along the way.

First, Victor E. paid a visit to NIU's president at Altgeld Hall, the most famous building on campus.

The president said, “Hello, Victor E.”
as the mascot walked through the door.

The next stop for Victor E. was East Lagoon. Victor E. fed the ducks with his friends from the NIU Pup Club.

The ducks were excited to see the friendly mascot and quacked, "Hello, Victor E."

Victor E. then made his way
to the Martin Luther King
Memorial Commons.

At this popular gathering spot,
Victor E. ran into fans coming from
Holmes Student Center on their way to
the football game.

Next, Victor E. made his way to the Recreation Center. He met up with friends heading to the football game.

Dressed in Huskie red and black, his
friends cheered, "Hello, Victor E."

Victor E. passed through the
Tent-A-Gate and FanFest tailgate
areas, where fans cheered,
"Hello, Victor E. Go, NIU!"

Victor E. then walked to the soccer field and track complex. The construction workers on site cheered, “Hello, Victor E.”

Next, Victor E. stopped by the Convocation Center to visit the NIU basketball team.

Inside the arena, the athletes cheered,
"Hello, Victor E."

Victor E. had one last stop to make before going to the stadium. He went to the Barsema Alumni and Visitors Center.

He ran into a group of NIU alumni. They remembered Victor E. from their days at NIU. They cheered, “Hello, again, Victor E.”

Finally, Victor E. arrived at Huskie Stadium, where he joined Huskie fans for the big game. Victor E., and his friend Spirit, sang the Huskie fight song as students chanted, "Forward, Together, Forward!"

Victor E. led the team onto the field through the Yordon Center tunnel. NIU fans cheered, “Go, Huskies!”

Victor E. was on the sideline when the Huskies scored their first touchdown! As the cheerleaders ran the H-U-S-K-I-E-S flags across the endzone, the quarterback yelled, “Touchdown, Victor E.”

Victor E. was back in the stands with his friends at halftime. The NIU Huskie Marching Band performed for fans. Everyone cheered, "Hello, Victor E."

The Huskies won the game! As the band played the fight song again, Victor E. went down to the field to give the coach a high-five. The coach yelled, "Great game, Victor E."

After the game, Victor E. celebrated the big win with excited NIU fans. Huskie fans cheered, "We did it, Victor E."

What a great day it had been at NIU!
As the mascot left the stadium, his fans
called, "Goodbye, Victor E."

Victor E. was tired. He walked home and went straight to bed.

Goodnight, Victor E.

PUP CLUB

If you know a young Huskie fan 8th grade or below interested in being a member of the Pup Club, you need to tell me, VICTOR E. HUSKIE!

I am recruiting as many NEW Pup Club Kids as possible for this upcoming year. The NIU Student-Athletes need our support! Young fans make a huge difference!

For Joining, members will receive:

- Free Admission to **ALL** regular season Huskie sporting events (including football, men's and women's basketball, volleyball, softball, baseball, gymnastics, and wrestling)
- An exclusive Pup Club t-shirt
- An official membership card
- A birthday card from me
- A surprise gift
- Invitations to other special events

If you have any questions, please contact my assistant, Jesse Seykora, at 815-753-0855 or at jseykora@niu.edu.

For more information about our products, please visit us online at www.mascotbooks.com.

For more information, please contact Mascot Books,
P.O. Box 220157, Chantilly, VA 20153-0157

ISBN: 978-1-932888-37-9

Printed in the United States.

www.mascotbooks.com

MASCOT BOOKS

www.mascotbooks.com

Title List

Major League Baseball

Boston Red Sox	Hello, *Wally*!	Jerry Remy
Boston Red Sox	*Wally The Green Monster* And His Journey Through *Red Sox Nation*!	Jerry Remy
Boston Red Sox	Coast to Coast with *Wally The Green Monster*	Jerry Remy
Boston Red Sox	A Season with *Wally The Green Monster*	Jerry Remy
Colorado Rockies	Hello, *Dinger*!	Aimee Aryal
Detroit Tigers	Hello, *Paws*!	Aimee Aryal
New York Yankees	Let's Go, *Yankees*!	Yogi Berra
New York Yankees	*Yankees Town*	Aimee Aryal
New York Mets	Hello, *Mr. Met*!	Rusty Staub
New York Mets	*Mr. Met* and his Journey Through the Big Apple	Aimee Aryal
St. Louis Cardinals	Hello, *Fredbird*!	Ozzie Smith
Philadelphia Phillies	Hello, *Phillie Phanatic*!	Aimee Aryal
Chicago Cubs	Let's Go, *Cubs*!	Aimee Aryal
Chicago White Sox	Let's Go, *White Sox*!	Aimee Aryal
Cleveland Indians	Hello, *Slider*!	Bob Feller
Seattle Mariners	Hello, *Mariner Moose*!	Aimee Aryal
Washington Nationals	Hello, *Screech*!	Aimee Aryal
Milwaukee Brewers	Hello, *Bernie Brewer*!	Aimee Aryal

Pro Football

Carolina Panthers	Let's Go, Panthers!	Aimee Aryal
Chicago Bears	Let's Go, Bears!	Aimee Aryal
Dallas Cowboys	How 'Bout Them Cowboys!	Aimee Aryal
Green Bay Packers	Go, Pack, Go!	Aimee Aryal
Kansas City Chiefs	Let's Go, Chiefs!	Aimee Aryal
Minnesota Vikings	Let's Go, Vikings!	Aimee Aryal
New York Giants	Let's Go, Giants!	Aimee Aryal
New York Jets	J-E-T-S! Jets, Jets, Jets!	Aimee Aryal
New England Patriots	Let's Go, Patriots!	Aimee Aryal
Pittsburgh Steelers	Here We Go Steelers!	Aimee Aryal
Seattle Seahawks	Let's Go, Seahawks!	Aimee Aryal
Washington Redskins	Hail To The Redskins!	Aimee Aryal

Basketball

Dallas Mavericks	Let's Go, Mavs!	Mark Cuban
Boston Celtics	Let's Go, Celtics!	Aimee Aryal

Other

Kentucky Derby	White Diamond Runs For The Roses	Aimee Aryal
Marine Corps Marathon	Run, Miles, Run!	Aimee Aryal

College

Alabama	Hello, Big Al!	Aimee Aryal
Alabama	Roll Tide!	Ken Stabler
Alabama	Big Al's Journey Through the Yellowhammer State	Aimee Aryal
Arizona	Hello, Wilbur!	Lute Olson
Arkansas	Hello, Big Red!	Aimee Aryal
Arkansas	Big Red's Journey Through the Razorback State	Aimee Aryal
Auburn	Hello, Aubie!	Aimee Aryal
Auburn	War Eagle!	Pat Dye
Auburn	Aubie's Journey Through the Yellowhammer State	Aimee Aryal
Boston College	Hello, Baldwin!	Aimee Aryal
Brigham Young	Hello, Cosmo!	LaVell Edwards
Cal - Berkeley	Hello, Oski!	Aimee Aryal
Clemson	Hello, Tiger!	Aimee Aryal
Clemson	Tiger's Journey Through the Palmetto State	Aimee Aryal
Colorado	Hello, Ralphie!	Aimee Aryal
Connecticut	Hello, Jonathan!	Aimee Aryal
Duke	Hello, Blue Devil!	Aimee Aryal
Florida	Hello, Albert!	Aimee Aryal
Florida State	Let's Go, 'Noles!	Aimee Aryal
Georgia	Hello, Hairy Dawg!	Aimee Aryal
Georgia	How 'Bout Them Dawgs!	Aimee Aryal
Georgia	Hairy Dawg's Journey Through the Peach State	Vince Dooley Vince Dooley
Georgia Tech	Hello, Buzz!	
Gonzaga	Spike, The Gonzaga Bulldog	Aimee Aryal Mike Pringle
Illinois	Let's Go, Illini!	
Indiana	Let's Go, Hoosiers!	Aimee Aryal
Iowa	Hello, Herky!	Aimee Aryal
Iowa State	Hello, Cy!	Aimee Aryal
James Madison	Hello, Duke Dog!	Amy DeLashmutt
Kansas	Hello, Big Jay!	Aimee Aryal
Kansas State	Hello, Willie!	Aimee Aryal
Kentucky	Hello, Wildcat!	Dan Walter
LSU	Hello, Mike!	Aimee Aryal
LSU	Mike's Journey Through the Bayou State	Aimee Aryal Aimee Aryal
Maryland	Hello, Testudo!	
Michigan	Let's Go, Blue!	Aimee Aryal
Michigan State	Hello, Sparty!	Aimee Aryal
Minnesota	Hello, Goldy!	Aimee Aryal
Mississippi	Hello, Colonel Rebel!	Aimee Aryal
Mississippi State	Hello, Bully!	Aimee Aryal
Missouri	Hello, Truman!	Aimee Aryal
Nebraska	Hello, Herbie Husker!	Todd Donoho
North Carolina	Hello, Rameses!	Aimee Aryal
North Carolina	Rameses' Journey Through the Tar Heel State	Aimee Aryal Aimee Aryal
North Carolina St.	Hello, Mr. Wuf!	
North Carolina St.	Mr. Wuf's Journey Through North Carolina	Aimee Aryal Aimee Aryal
Notre Dame	Let's Go, Irish!	
Ohio State	Hello, Brutus!	Aimee Aryal
Ohio State	Brutus' Journey	Aimee Aryal
Oklahoma	Let's Go, Sooners!	Aimee Aryal
Oklahoma State	Hello, Pistol Pete!	Aimee Aryal
Oregon	Go Ducks!	Aimee Aryal
Oregon State	Hello, Benny the Beaver!	Aimee Aryal
Penn State	Hello, Nittany Lion!	Aimee Aryal
Penn State	We Are Penn State!	Aimee Aryal
Purdue	Hello, Purdue Pete!	Joe Paterno
Rutgers	Hello, Scarlet Knight!	Aimee Aryal
South Carolina	Hello, Cocky!	Aimee Aryal
South Carolina	Cocky's Journey Through the Palmetto State	Aimee Aryal Aimee Aryal
So. California	Hello, Tommy Trojan!	
Syracuse	Hello, Otto!	Aimee Aryal
Tennessee	Hello, Smokey!	Aimee Aryal
Tennessee	Smokey's Journey Through the Volunteer State	Aimee Aryal Aimee Aryal
Texas	Hello, Hook 'Em!	
Texas	Hook 'Em's Journey Through the Lone Star State	Aimee Aryal Aimee Aryal
Texas A & M	Howdy, Reveille!	
Texas A & M	Reveille's Journey Through the Lone Star State	Aimee Aryal Aimee Aryal
Texas Tech	Hello, Masked Rider!	
UCLA	Hello, Joe Bruin!	Aimee Aryal
Virginia	Hello, CavMan!	Aimee Aryal
Virginia Tech	Hello, Hokie Bird!	Aimee Aryal
Virginia Tech	Yea, It's Hokie Game Day!	Aimee Aryal
Virginia Tech	Hokie Bird's Journey Through Virginia	Frank Beamer Aimee Aryal
Wake Forest	Hello, Demon Deacon!	
Washington	Hello, Harry the Husky!	Aimee Aryal
Washington State	Hello, Butch!	Aimee Aryal
West Virginia	Hello, Mountaineer!	Aimee Aryal
Wisconsin	Hello, Bucky!	Aimee Aryal
Wisconsin	Bucky's Journey Through the Badger State	Aimee Aryal Aimee Aryal

Order online at **mascotbooks.com** using promo code " **free**" to receive **FREE SHIPPING!**

More great titles coming soon!

info@mascotbooks.com